Introducción a los padres

We Both Read es la primera serie de libros diseñada para invitar a padres e hijos a compartir la lectura de un cuento, por turnos y en voz alta. Esta "lectura compartida" —que se ha desarrollado en conjunto con especialistas en primeras lecturas— invita a los padres a leer los textos más complejos en la página de la izquierda. Luego, les toca a los niños leer las páginas de la derecha, que contienen textos más sencillos, escritos específicamente para primeros lectores.

Leer en voz alta es una de las actividades más importantes que los padres comparten con sus hijos para ayudarlos a desarrollar la lectura. Sin embargo, *We Both Read* no es solo leerle *a* un niño, sino que les permite a los padres leer *con* el niño. *We Both Read* es más poderoso y efectivo porque combina dos elementos claves del aprendizaje: "demostración" (el padre lee) y "aplicación" (el niño lee). El resultado no es solo que el niño aprende a leer más rápido, ¡sino que ambos disfrutan y se enriquecen con esta experiencia!

Sería más útil si usted lee el libro completo y en voz alta la primera vez, y luego invita a su niño a participar en una segunda lectura. En algunos libros, las palabras más difíciles se presentan por primera vez en **negritas** en el texto del padre. Señalar o conversar sobre estas palabras ayudará a su niño a familiarizarse con estas y a ampliar su vocabulario. También notará que el ícono "lee el padre" ⊚ precede el texto del padre y el ícono de "lee el niño" ⊚ precede el texto del niño.

Lo invitamos a compartir y a relacionarse con su niño mientras leen el libro juntos. Si su hijo tiene dificultad, usted puede mencionar algunas cosas que lo ayuden. "Decir cada sonido" es bueno, pero puede que esto no funcione con todas las palabras. Los niños pueden hallar pistas en las palabras del cuento, en el contexto de las oraciones e incluso de las imágenes. Algunos cuentos incluyen patrones y rimas que los ayudarán. También le podría ser útil a su niño tocar las palabras con su dedo mientras leen para conectar mejor las palabras habladas con las palabras impresas.

¡Al compartir los libros de *We Both Read*, usted y su hijo vivirán juntos la fascinante aventura de la lectura! Es una manera divertida y fácil de animar y ayudar a su niño a leer —¡y una maravillosa manera de preparar a su niño para disfrutar de la lectura durante toda su vida!

WE BOTH READ®

Parent's Introduction

We Both Read is the first series of books designed to invite parents and children to share the reading of a story by taking turns reading aloud. This "shared reading" innovation, which was developed with reading education specialists, invites parents to read the more complex text and storyline on the left-hand pages. Then children can be encouraged to read the right-hand pages, which feature less complex text and storyline, specifically written for the beginning reader.

Reading aloud is one of the most important activities parents can share with their child to assist in his or her reading development. However, *We Both Read* goes beyond reading *to* a child and allows parents to share the reading *with* a child. *We Both Read* is so powerful and effective because it combines two key elements in learning: "modeling" (the parent reads) and "doing" (the child reads). The result is not only faster reading development for the child but a much more enjoyable and enriching experience for both!

You may find it helpful to read the entire book aloud yourself the first time, then invite your child to participate in the second reading. In some books, a few more difficult words will first be introduced in the parent's text, distinguished with **bold lettering**. Pointing out, and even discussing, these words will help familiarize your child with them and help to build your child's vocabulary. Also, note that a "talking parent" icon ☺ precedes the parent's text and a "talking child" icon ☺ precedes the child's text.

We encourage you to share and interact with your child as you read the book together. If your child is having difficulty, you might want to mention a few things to help him or her. "Sounding out" is good, but it will not work with all words. Children can pick up clues about the words they are reading from the story, the context of the sentence, or even the pictures. Some stories have rhyming patterns that might help. It might also help them to touch the words with their finger as they read, to better connect the spoken words and the printed words.

Sharing the *We Both Read* books together will engage you and your child in an interactive adventure in reading! It is a fun and easy way to encourage and help your child to read—and a wonderful way to start your child off on a lifetime of reading enjoyment!

Frank and the Tiger
Sapi y el tigre
A We Both Read® Book

We Both Read® is a trademark of Treasure Bay, Inc.

Published by Treasure Bay, Inc.
P.O. Box 119
Novato, CA 94948 USA

Printed in Singapore

Library of Congress Catalog Card Number: 2012955734

Paperback ISBN: 978-1-60115-058-5

We Both Read® Books
Patent No. 5,957,693

Visit us online at:
www.WeBothRead.com

PR-11-13

WE BOTH READ®

Dos leemos

Frank and the Tiger
Sapi y el tigre

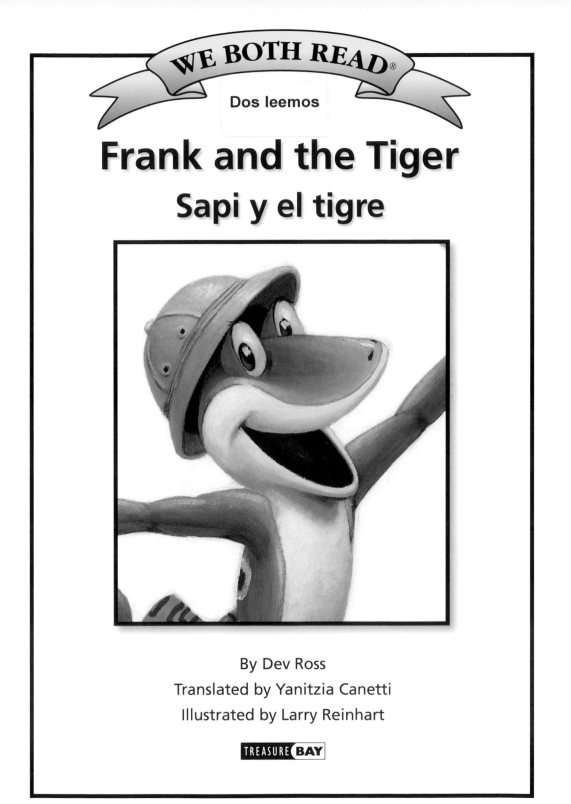

By Dev Ross
Translated by Yanitzia Canetti
Illustrated by Larry Reinhart

TREASURE BAY

One day, Frank put on an old hat. It looked like a jungle explorer hat, so Frank asked Mikey, "Do you want to look for wild animals with me?"
Mikey answered, . . .

Un día Sapi se puso un viejo sombrero. Parecía un sombrero de explorador, así que le preguntó a Rito:
—*¿Quieres ir conmigo a buscar animales salvajes?*
Rito le contestó: . . .

 "No!"

—¡No!

Suddenly they heard a noise. Mikey said, "I hope it's not a lion!"

Then a face peeked through the bushes.

"**It is** not a lion," said Frank.

De repente escucharon un ruido.

—¡Espero que no sea un león! —dijo Rito.

Entonces una cara se asomó entre los arbustos.

*—No **es** un león —dijo Rito.*

"It is a boy!"

—¡Es un niño!

The boy called out, "Tiger! Where are you, Tiger?"
"Oh, dear," said Frank. "**He is** looking for his lost tiger."

—¡Tigre! ¿Dónde estás, Tigre? —gritaba el niño.
—Ay, amigo —dijo Sapi—. ***Él está*** buscando a su tigre extraviado.

"**He is** sad."

—*Él está* triste.

Frank did not like seeing the boy so sad. "Let's find his lost tiger for him," he said. And off he went.

A Sapi no le gustaba ver al niño tan triste.
*—Vamos a buscar a su tigre perdido —dijo. Y se marchó **salta** que salta.*

Hop, hop, hop!

¡Salta, salta, salta!

Mikey did not want to look for a tiger. But what if the tiger wanted to look for Mikey? Mikey began to **run**, racing to catch up to Frank.

*Rito no quería ir a buscar a un tigre. Pero, ¿y si el tigre lo buscaba a él? Rito echó a **correr** para alcanzar a Sapi.*

Run, run, run!

*¡A **correr**, correr, correr!*

Frank spotted something. It looked like a tail. He crept up quietly to see if **it was** the tiger.

*Sapi vio algo. Parecía una cola. Se deslizó sin hacer ruido para ver si **era** el tigre.*

It was not.

No *era.*

Mikey did not want to look for the **tiger** anymore. He wanted to go home. Then suddenly, there it was in front of him.

*Rito no quería buscar más al **tigre**. Quería irse a casa. Entonces, de repente, ahí estaba frente a él.*

The **tiger**!!!

¡¡¡El **tigre**!!!

Mikey was scared, but Frank was brave. "**Come,** tiger," he said, "we are taking you home."

The tiger did not move. It was a toy! Now Mikey was brave too. He said, . . .

Rito estaba asustado, pero Sapi era valiente.

*—**Ven,** tigre—le dijo—, te llevaremos a casa.*

El tigre no se movía. ¡Era de juguete! Así que Rito también se sintió valiente y dijo: . . .

"Come, tiger!"

—¡Ven, tigre!

Then they heard loud barking. They turned around to see a **dog** running right toward them! Frank held up his hand and shouted, . . .

*Entonces oyeron ladridos. ¡Se dieron la vuelta y vieron a un **perro** que corría directo hacia ellos! Sapi levantó la mano y gritó: . . .*

"Stop, **dog**, stop!"

—¡Para, **perro**, para!

The dog did not stop. He **ran** past Mikey and Frank! He picked up the tiger in his mouth and kept running.

El perro no se detuvo. **Corría** *rápido, ¡y pasó corriendo a Rito y Sapi! Agarró al tigre con la boca y siguió corriendo.*

He **ran** and ran!

¡Él **corría** y corría!

"We have to rescue the tiger!" shouted Frank. "We have to bring him back to the little boy."

Mikey knew that Frank was right. "**Here** comes the dog again," said Frank.

—¡*Tenemos que rescatar al tigre!* —*exclamó Sapi*—. *Tenemos que devolvérselo al niñito.*

Rito sabía que Sapi tenía razón.

—***Aquí*** *viene el perro otra vez* —*dijo Sapi.*

"And **here** we go!"

—¡Y **aquí** vamos!

Frank grabbed the dog's tail with one hand and Mikey with the other. **"This is great,"** said Frank as they were pulled into the air.

*Sapi agarró la cola del perro con una mano y con la otra a Rito. —¡**Qué fabuloso!** —decía Sapi mientras se balanceaban en el aire.*

 *"This is great!"*

—¡Qué fabuloso!

Frank held tightly to Mikey's hand. Soon Mikey was enjoying the ride too. He shouted, . . .

*Sapi sujetaba fuerte la mano de Rito. Enseguida Rito comenzó a disfrutar también de la **diversión** y gritó: . . .*

"Yes! It is fun!"

—¡Sí! ¡Qué **diversión!**

The dog stopped and Frank let go of its tail. Frank grabbed the tiger. "Let go," he told the dog as he began to **tug**.

*El perro se detuvo y Sapi se soltó de su cola. Sapi agarró al tigre. —¡Suéltalo! —le dijo al perro mientras comenzaba a **jalar** el tigre.*

Tug, tug, tug!

¡A *jalar*, jalar, jalar!

The dog was strong. "What can we do?" said Frank. "He won't let go!"

"Your hat!" yelled Mikey. "**Throw** your hat, Frank!"

El perro era fuerte. —¿Qué podemos hacer? —dijo Sapi—. ¡Él no lo suelta!

*—Tu sombrero —gritó Rito—, ¡**tíralo**, Sapi!*

 **"Throw it!"**

—¡*Tíralo!*

Frank threw his hat. It flew through the air like a flying saucer. The dog started to run after it.

Sapi tiró su sombrero. Voló por el aire como un platillo volador. El perró echó a correr detrás de este.

Run, dog, run!

¡Corre, perro, corre!

Now it was time to take the tiger back to the boy. Frank and Mikey dragged it to his door. Then they heard footsteps. **Was** it the boy?

*Ya era hora de devolverle el tigre al niño. Sapi y Rito lo arrastraron hasta su puerta. Entonces escucharon pasos. ¿**Era** el niño?*

It **was** the boy!

¡Era el niño!

The boy saw his tiger. He gave it a big hug. Then the big dog came running in. The boy threw the tiger and shouted, . . .

El niño miró a su tigre y le dio un gran abrazo. En eso llegó corriendo el perro grande. El niño lanzó el tigre al aire y gritó: . . .

"Go, boy! Get it!"

¡Dale, ve tras él!

Frank and Mikey had rescued the tiger from the dog. Now the boy was giving it back to him!

Frank laughed. Mikey laughed too! It was **funny**.

Sapi y Rito habían rescatado al tigre del perro. ¡Pero ahora el niño se lo daba otra vez!

*Sapi se reía. ¡Rito también se reía! Daba **risa**.*

It was **funny**!

*¡Qué **risa** me da!*

 "Come on," said Frank. "**Let's go** and rescue the tiger again!"

"Okay," said Mikey.

—Vamos —dijo Sapi—. ¡**Vamos** a rescatar al tigre otra vez!

—De acuerdo —dijo Rito.

 "Let's go!"

—¡Vamos!

If you liked **Frank and the Tiger,** here is another
We Both Read® Book you are sure to enjoy!

*Si te gustó leer **Sapi y el tigre,** ¡seguramente disfrutarás al leer
este otro libro de la serie We Both Read®!*

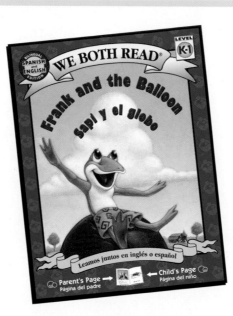

Frank the frog is carried off into the sky hanging from a balloon. At first this seems like an exciting adventure, but soon Frank just wants to go home.

Sapi, el sapo, se va flotando en el aire en un globo. Al principio, le parece una aventura emocionante, pero poco después, Sapi solo desea regresar a casa.

To see all the We Both Read® books that are available,
just go online to **www.WeBothRead.com.**

*Para ver todos los libros disponibles de la serie We Both Read®,
visita nuestra página web: **www.WeBothRead.com.***